JESSIE ELLIOT IS A BIG CHICKEN

JESSIE ELLIOT IS A BIG CHICKEN

WRITTEN AND
ILLUSTRATED BY

ELISE GRAVEL

 • NEW YORK

PUBLISHED BY ROARING BROOK PRESS
ROARING BROOK PRESS IS A DIVISION OF HOLTZBRINCK
PUBLISHING HOLDINGS LIMITED PARTNERSHIP
175 FIFTH AVENUE, NEW YORK, NEW YORK 10010
mackids.com

LIBRARY OF CONGRESS CATALOGING-IN-PUBLICATION DATA

Gravel, Elise author, illustrator
 Jessie Elliot is a big chicken / written and illustrated by Elise
Gravel
     pages cm
 Summary: "During the summer before high school, Jessie Elliot vows to
never change her fun-filled, dorky ways -- that is until her best friend
starts hanging out with the cool kids" -- provided by publisher.
 ISBN 978-1-59643-741-8 (hardback)
[1. Best friends--Fiction. 2. Friendship--Fiction. 3. Humorous stories.]
I. Title
  PZ7.G7728Je 2014
  [Fic]--dc23

ROARING BROOK PRESS BOOKS MAY BE PURCHASED FOR
BUSINESS OR PROMOTIONAL USE. FOR INFORMATION
PLEASE CONTACT MACMILLAN CORPORATE AND PREMIUM
SALES DEPARTMENT AT (800) 221-7945 x5442 OR BY EMAIL AT
SPECIALMARKETS@MACMILLAN.COM.

FIRST EDITION 2014

PRINTED IN CHINA BY TOPPAN LEEFUNG PRINTING LTD.,
DONGGUAN CITY, GUANGDONG PROVINCE

TO MARIE H,
MY BFF

JESSIE ELLIOT

NERD EXTRAORDINAIRE ★ ★ ★

WEIRD UNIDENTIFIED DOG-LIKE CREATURE

I WISH I HAD COWBOY BOOTS LIKE THESE

MY NAME IS JESSIE
ELLIOT AND THIS IS
MY LAST SUMMER AS A

CHILD.

AT THE END OF THE SUMMER, I WILL GO TO HOCHELAGA HIGH.
DIRTY SOCK FUMES
NOT A SINGLE TREE
WINDOWS JUST BIG ENOUGH TO LET RATS IN
HOCHELAGA HIG
CATTLE TRUCK
CATTLE TRUCK
STUDENTS ENTRANCE

THE KIDS AT HOCHELAGA HIGH LOOK LIKE BORED WANNABES. THEY HANG AROUND WITH SULTRY FACES, CALL EACH OTHER NAMES, PAINT THEIR EYES LIKE RACCOONS, AND SMOKE CIGARETTES, IMAGINING I GUESS THAT THEY LOOK LIKE ROCKSTARS. MAYBE THERE'S SOME KIND OF CHEMICAL REACTION IN HUMAN BRAINS THAT'S TRIGGERED WHEN WE TURN THIRTEEN THAT MAKE US INSTANTLY STUPID.

EGG-HEADED TOUGH GUYS
OH-SO-REBEL
GALLONS OF MASCARA
PERPETUAL POUTS
LITERS OF HAIR SPRAY
WOOL HATS IN SUMMER

STUPID LiKE

SHE USED TO HANG OUT WITH US, BUT NOW THAT SHE'S IN HiGH SCHOOL, SHE THiNKS SHE'S SO COOL WITH HER TiNY TANK TOPS AND HER PSEUDO-PUNK HAiRDO.

NOW SHE HANGS OUT WITH A BUNCH OF FREAKS AND SHE SNICKERS WHEN SHE SEES ME.

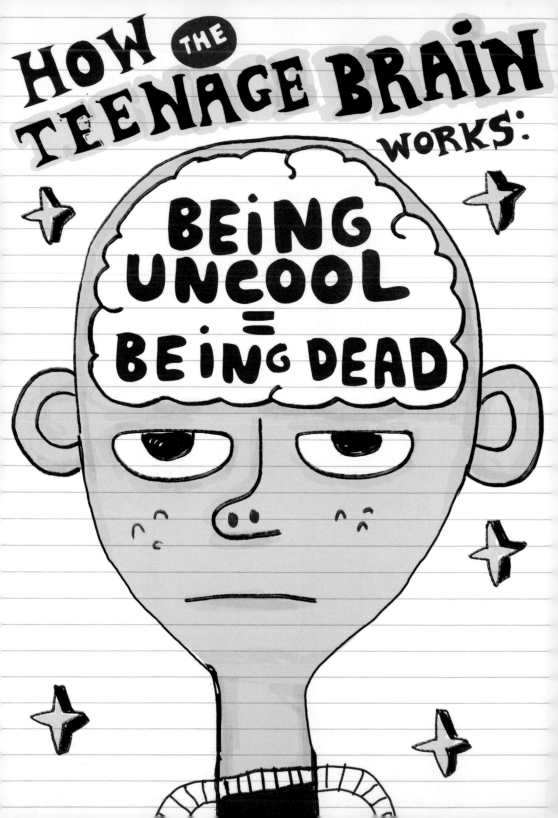

TOP 10

REASONS WHY THERE'S

NO WAY

I'LL EVER BE SUPERCOOL IN HIGH SCHOOL:

1- I READ TOO MUCH
2- I STILL HAVE A MY LITTLE PONIES
   COLLECTION
3- MY PARENTS WON'T GET ME
   RED COWBOY BOOTS
4- MY MOM STILL CUTS MY HAIR
5- I LIKE TO PLAY SCRABBLE
6- THERE'S A UNICORN ON MY PENCIL CASE
7- I DON'T SMOKE
8- I HAVE DUMBO EARS
9- I GO TO BED AT 9:30
10- I'M SCARED OF EVERYTHING

AT LEAST MY BEST FRIENDS ARE
COMING WITH ME TO HOCHELAGA HIGH:

JULiE

JULiE HAS BEEN MY BEST FRiEND FOREVER.
SHE'S LiKE MY SiSTER. SHE'S HiLARiOUS.
SHE'S THE BEST AT MiMiCKiNG VOiCES AND
PEOPLE, AND SHE HAS A FUNNY SPACE
BETWEEN HER FRONT TEETH THAT SHE CAN
WHiSTLE THROUGH.

EVERYBODY LiKES HER.

THIS IS HER DOING THE

MOONWALK.

JULIE AND I, WE'RE LIKE MENTAL TWINS. TOGETHER, WE ORGANIZE INSULT

WE HAVE AN OFFICIAL

club charter

THINGS WE HATE

- DODGEBALL
- PEOPLE CRUNCHING CARROTS IN A SILENT ROOM
- TEACHERS WITH BAD BREATH
- BEING HUMAN BEINGS INSTEAD OF COYOTES
- ISABELLE LEMOINE
- FRACTIONS
- TURTLENECK SWEATERS
- PEOPLE SAYING "OH-MY-GOD" ALL THE TIME
- THE WITCH

THINGS WE LIKE

- PICKING OUR SCABS
- BEING OVERLY DRAMATIC!!!
- PAINTING REALISTIC THIRD EYES ON OUR FOREHEADS
- SINGING REALLY LOUDLY IN PUBLIC
- STUPID CATS
- TATTOOING OUR WHOLE ARMS WITH BIC PENS
- OBSESSING OVER COMPLETELY USELESS STUFF
- PRACTICING SILLY BREAKDANCE MOVES

WE ALSO LIKE WEIRD ANIMALS, LIKE JULIE'S DOG, NORMAL. HE WAS RESCUED FROM A SHELTER AND HE CAN'T BARK BECAUSE HIS VOCAL CORDS WERE CUT, SO HE'S ALWAYS BARKING IN SILENCE, WHICH IS PRETTY PATHETIC.

ASIDE FROM BARKING SILENTLY, HIS
MOST INTERESTING ACHIEVEMENT IS DRAGGING
HIS BUTT ON THE GROUND OVER VERY
LONG DISTANCES TO SCRATCH IT.
HE'LL CERTAINLY WIN THE FIRST PLACE
IF THERE EVER IS AN

INTERNATIONAL CANINE BUTT-SCRATCHING MARATHON!

WHEE!

IF WE DON'T BECOME COYOTES OR VAMPIRES
WHEN WE GROW UP, JULIE AND I WILL OPEN A PET
PSYCHIATRY CLINIC. I'M SURE WE'LL HAVE
LOTS OF FUN!

JULIE AND I ARE ALSO WRITING A COMIC BOOK.
I DO THE DRAWINGS. OUR HERO IS CALLED

SUPER-PICKLE FIGHTS EVIL TEACHERS, OUR WORST
ENEMY ISABELLE LEMOINE, THE WITCH (MORE ABOUT
HER LATER), AND ALL SORTS OF ANNOYING PEOPLE.

SOME OTHER KIDS FROM THE NEIGHBORHOOD
ARE ALSO GOING TO HOCHELAGA HIGH:

#1 EXPERT IN CHEAP
HORROR MOVIES, SCARY
STORIES AND EVERYTHING
GORY.

MIKE SAYS THAT IF YOU'RE
NOT SUPER-TOUGH IN HIGH-
SCHOOL, OTHER KIDS WILL TAKE
ADVANTAGE OF YOU. HE SAYS
ONE OF HIS COUSINS WAS
ACTUALLY FORCED TO TAKE DRUGS
BY SKINHEADS WITH KNIVES,
AND THAT HE OVERDOSED AND
NOW HE DROOLS AND BEGS FOR
MONEY ON SAINT-CATHERINE
STREET.

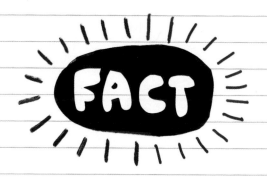

MIKE ALWAYS HAS ONE COUSIN
OR ANOTHER TO ILLUSTRATE HIS
CRAZY STORIES.

SOME OF
MiKE'S COUSINS

MATT

DROWNED IN HIS
GLASS OF COKE

CHARLES

HAD AN INGROWN
TOENAIL THAT EXPLODED

LUKE

ATE AND THEN BARFED
A LIVE FLY

FRED

WAS BORN WITH
4 EXTRA NIPPLES

THERE'S ALSO BEN, THE LOVE OF MY
LIFE (BUT HE DOESN'T KNOW IT YET).
WE'VE BEEN FRIENDS SINCE WE WERE 4.

BEN IS THE ONLY KID I KNOW WHO'S
COOL WITHOUT EVER TRYING TO BE.
HE DOESN'T TALK MUCH, THOUGH.
HE PLAYS SPORTS AND HE HAS
GOOD GRADES AND HE TELLS REALLY
GOOD JOKES, BUT TRYING TO HAVE
A CONVERSATION WITH HIM IS LIKE
TRYING TO PLAY PING-PONG WITH
A MUSHROOM.

ONCE, WE WALKED HOME FROM
SCHOOL TOGETHER AND THE ONLY
WORDS HE SAID TO ME WERE
"WANT SOME GUM?"

SOMETIMES I THINK THAT HIS
SILENCE MAKES HIM REALLY
MYSTERIOUS AND DEEP, BUT
SOMETIMES, JUST SOMETIMES,
I WONDER IF MAYBE HE
DOESN'T HAVE ANYTHING
INTERESTING TO SAY.

VERY MYSTERIOUS
GUM

QUESTION:

WHAT IF HE'S JUST A LITTLE BIT DUMB?

EVEN WITH ALL THESE
FRIENDS AROUND, I'M
STILL SCARED OF HIGH
SCHOOL.

HOW CAN I EVER BE
TOUGH ENOUGH TO FACE
A BUNCH OF STONED
SKINHEADS? I'M NOT
EVEN TOUGH ENOUGH
TO GO TO THE STICKS
ALONE.

THE STICKS

IS A VACANT LOT AT THE END OF OUR
STREET. THERE'S AN OLD PARKING LOT
WHERE WE CAN PLAY SOCCER, AND
AN ABANDONED PICK-UP TRUCK WHERE
YOU CAN SIT IF YOU'RE NOT AFRAID
OF BUGS AND SPIDERS. THERE'S ALSO A
A TINY POND WITH CRAYFISH IN IT,
AND ENOUGH TREES TO PLAY HIDE-AND-
SEEK. IT'S LIKE BEING IN THE COUNTRY,
BUT RIGHT IN THE MIDDLE OF THE CITY.

THE STICKS IS A COOL PLACE TO HANG
AROUND IN DAYTIME, BUT IT GETS
REALLY SCARY AT NIGHT. THERE'S A
FIRE PIT IN THE BUSHES WITH
EMPTY BEER BOTTLES AROUND IT,
AND SOMETIMES DIRTY UNDERWEAR
AND SLEEPING BAGS.

THERE ARE SOME ANIMALS IN THE STICKS
AS WELL. WE SAW A HARE ONCE, SOME RACCOONS,
EVEN A SKUNK. THEY COME THROUGH THE OLD
RAILROAD TRACKS NEARBY AND THEY HIDE
UNDER PEOPLE'S PORCHES AND TOOLSHEDS. WHAT
I WOULD REALLY LIKE TO SEE IS A COYOTE.
I LOVE COYOTES BECAUSE THEY'RE AS CLEVER AS
DOGS AND AS INDEPENDENT AS CATS. IN A
PREVIOUS LIFE, I'M SURE I WAS A COYOTE.

OTHER ANIMALS ENCOUNTERED AT THE STICKS:

TEENAGE BOYS.

ONLY TEENAGERS DARE TO GO TO THE
STICKS AFTER DARK. THEY HANG OUT
AROUND THE PICKUP AND SMOKE AND
DRINK AND BELCH. SOMETIMES THERE'S
A GIRL OR TWO WITH THEM. WE LIKE TO
SPY ON THEM FROM MIKE'S BACKYARD; I
THINK THEY'RE ALL PRETTY

CREEPY.

ONCE, I SAW ISABELLE LEMOINE WITH THEM.

IN A PREVIOUS LIFE, I WAS A COYOTE.

OTHER THINGS I MIGHT HAVE BEEN IN PREVIOUS LIVES:

A YETI

A CRAZY NUN

A SHRIMP

THERE WAS A WOMAN WE CALLED "THE WITCH" WHO LIVED IN A HOUSE RIGHT NEXT TO THE STICKS. SHE WAS MEAN AND SHE NEVER SMILED. SHE HATED IT WHEN WE PLAYED IN THE PARKING LOT BECAUSE SHE SAID WE MADE TOO MUCH NOISE.

WHEN SHE SAW US, SHE ALWAYS CAME OUT TO YELL AT US. SHE EVEN CALLED THE POLICE A FEW TIMES. SHE ACTED AS IF WE WERE DANGEROUS AX MURDERERS OR SOMETHING. BUT EVEN THE COPS THOUGHT THAT SHE WAS ANNOYING AND WASTING THEIR TIME. THEY MADE FUN OF HER.

THE WITCH THOUGHT SHE WAS THE ONLY ONE
WITH A RIGHT TO THE STICKS. SHE HAD TWO
UGLY LITTLE DOGS AND SHE TRAINED THEM
IN THE PARKING LOT. SHE NEVER LET US PET
THE DOGS BECAUSE SHE SAID IT DISTRACTED THEM.

FROU-FROU

SOME EQUALLY STUPID NAME

ONCE, SHE CAUGHT BEN PLAYING
HOCKEY IN THE PARKING LOT AND
SHE CONFISCATED HIS STICK.

DANGEROUS
WEAPON OF
DOG-DISTRACTION

WE ALL HATED HER, SO WE DECIDED
TO FORM AN ANTI-WITCH CLUB. BEN
WAS THE CAPTAIN (THANKS TO
HIS MARTYR STATUS FOLLOWING THE
HOCKEY STICK INCIDENT). ALL THE
KIDS IN THE NEIGHBORHOOD WERE
ALLOWED TO JOIN. BEN WOULD
NEVER REJECT ANY KID.

EVEN THE
WEE SNOTTY
ONES

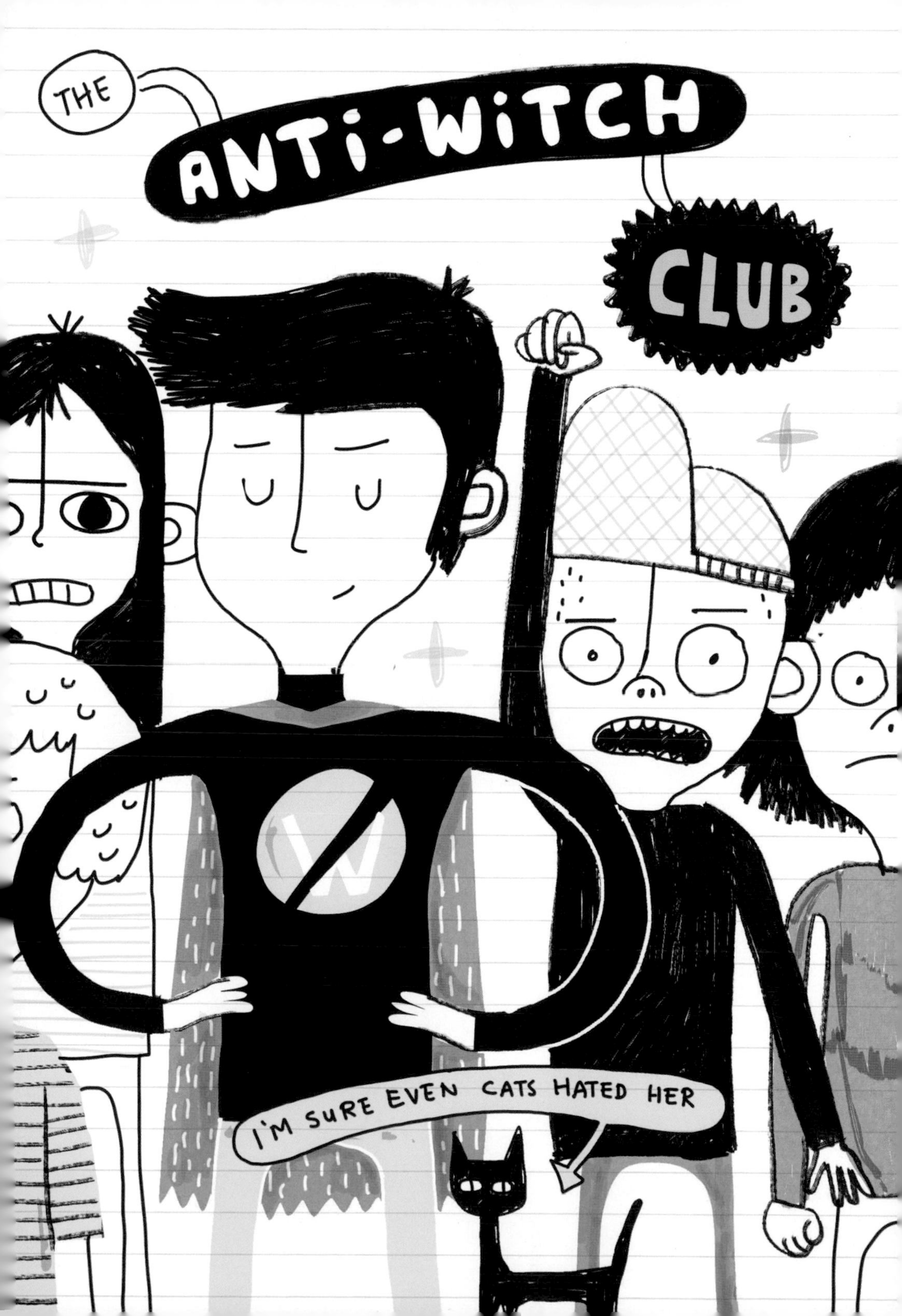
THE
ANTI-WITCH
CLUB
I'M SURE EVEN CATS HATED HER

OF COURSE, THE
WITCH AND BEN ARE
MAJOR CHARACTERS
IN OUR SUPER-PICKLE

COMICS.

SOMETIMES, WE'VE BEEN REALLY MEAN.
ONCE, MIKE FILLED A PIZZA BOX
WITH DOG POO, LEFT IT AT THE
WITCH'S DOOR, RANG, AND RAN
AWAY. WE THOUGHT WE WERE
BEING AWFULLY FUNNY.

LAST SPRING, I SAW THAT THE WITCH
HAD LEFT HER RAIN BOOTS OUTSIDE
THE GARAGE, AND I PEED IN ONE
OF THEM. FOR WEEKS AFTER THAT,
I WAS THE MOST POPULAR KID ON
THE STREET.

WHEN I THINK ABOUT IT NOW, I FEEL
ASHAMED. SOMETIMES, I DO STUPID
THINGS LIKE THAT, JUST TO
IMPRESS PEOPLE.

TWO WEEKS AGO, WHILE WE WERE IN THE STICKS
PLAYING SOCCER, AN AMBULANCE CAME AND
TOOK THE WITCH AWAY. WE WATCHED FROM THE
CURB. THE PARAMEDICS ROLLED A STRETCHER
IN FRONT OF THE HOUSE. HER FACE WAS GRAY.
SHE DIDN'T LOOK AT US.

THE NEXT DAY, THE WITCH'S SISTER CAME
AND TOOK THE DOGS
AWAY. SHE TALKED
TO MIKE'S MOM.

SINCE THEN, I HAVE TROUBLE FALLING
ASLEEP.

I KEEP THINKING THAT THE WITCH
WILL COME BACK AND PUNISH ME
FOR ALL THE TRICKS I PLAYED ON HER.
ESPECIALLY THE BOOT PART. I WISH
I HAD NEVER DONE THAT.

IN MY DREAMS, THE WITCH
COMES BACK AND YELLS AT
ME:

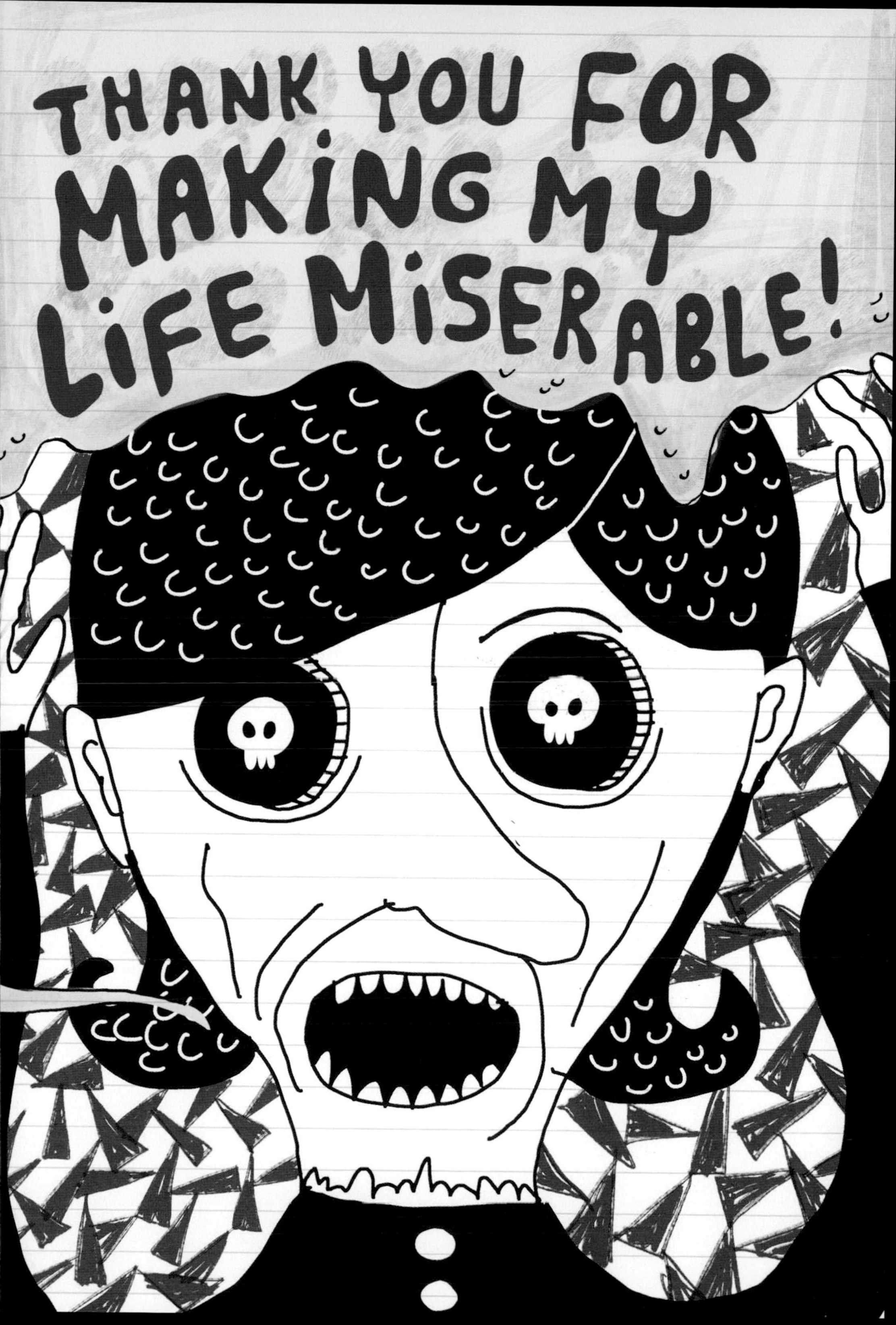
THANK YOU FOR MAKING MY LIFE MISERABLE!

NOBODY PLAYS IN THE
STICKS MUCH ANYMORE.
EVEN THE CREEPY
BOYS WITH MULLETS
HANG OUT AT THE MALL
NOW INSTEAD.

TANYA SAYS THAT ONE DAY
SHE'LL TAKE A SLEEPING BAG
AND SLEEP IN THE STICKS
NEXT TO THE FIRE PIT
BECAUSE SHE WANTS TO MEET
THE WITCH'S GHOST.

SOMETIMES I WISH I WAS
MORE LIKE TANYA. EVERY-
THING SEEMS LIKE A GAME
TO HER.

BUT I'M NOT AT ALL
LIKE TANYA. IN FACT,
WE'RE AS SIMILAR
AS A POODLE AND
A HUSKY DOG.

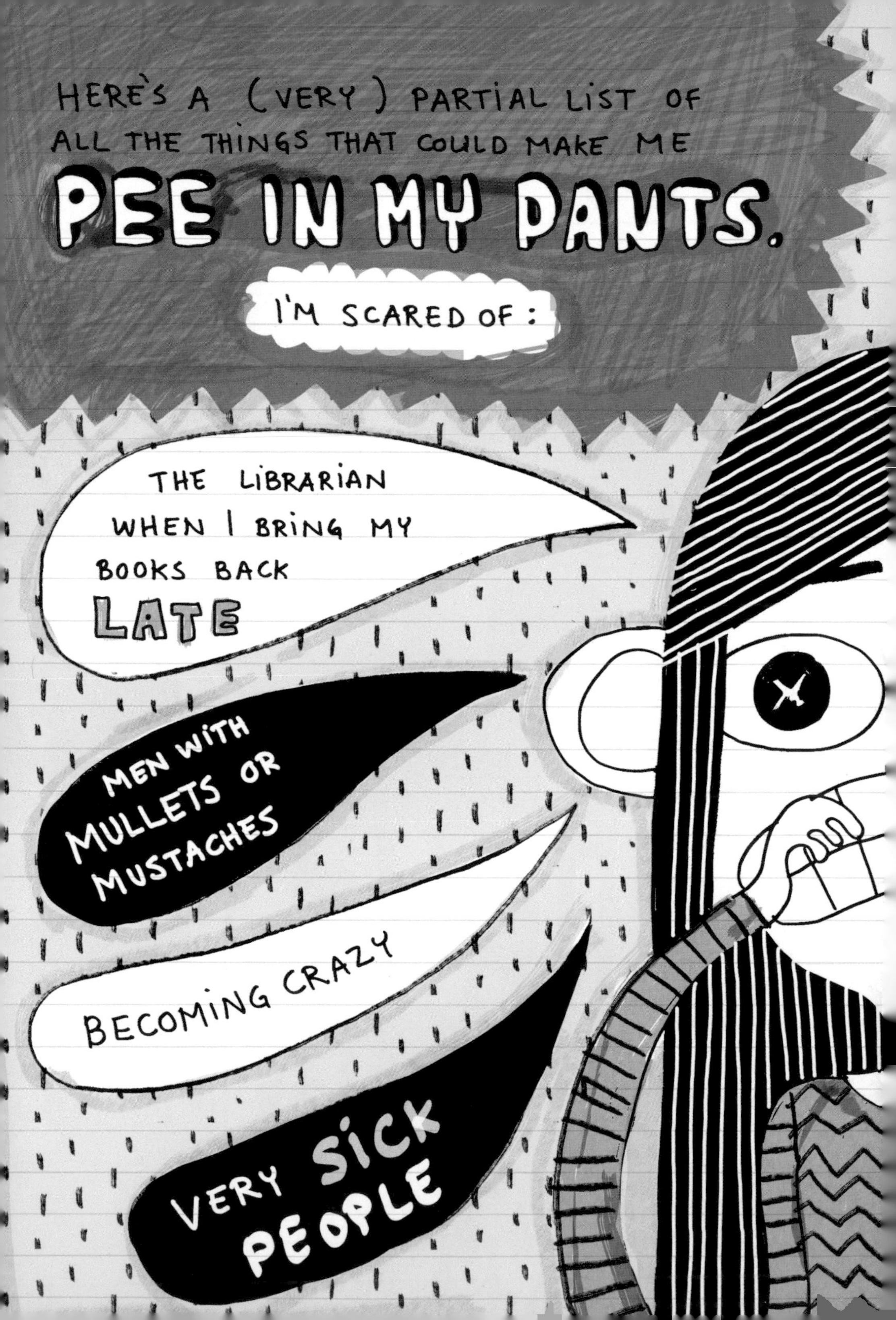
HERE'S A (VERY) PARTIAL LIST OF ALL THE THINGS THAT COULD MAKE ME
PEE IN MY PANTS.
I'M SCARED OF:
THE LIBRARIAN WHEN I BRING MY BOOKS BACK LATE
MEN WITH MULLETS OR MUSTACHES
BECOMING CRAZY
VERY SICK PEOPLE

BAD GRADES
CANCER
GETTING LOST IN THE SUBWAY
FALLING FLAT ON MY FACE IN FRONT OF EVERYBODY
PEOPLE FINDING OUT THAT I STILL WEAR STRAWBERRY SHORTCAKE UNDERWEAR
DOLLS WITH BATTERY-POWERED VOICES
BEING A REJECT
CLOWNS

MY WIMPINESS IS PAINFUL
ENOUGH AS IT IS, BUT LATELY
IT ALMOST CAUSED ME TO
LOSE MY BEST FRIEND.

EVERY SUMMER, JULIE INVITES
ME TO HER COTTAGE UP NORTH.

THERE'S A LAKE, AND IT'S ALMOST
200 HUNDRED FEET DEEP NEAR
THE DIVING ROCK. THE WATER
IS SO COLD IN JUNE THAT WE
FEEL ALL DIZZY AND LIGHT-
HEADED WHEN WE COME OUT.

SAMPLE FROM THE COTTAGE LIBRARY

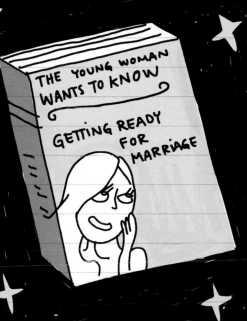

HERE'S THE BOOK I LIKE BEST:

READER'S DIGEST

MYSTERIES OF THE UNEXPLAINED

MYSTERIES OF THE UNEXPLAINED

CRAZY KINGS AND QUEENS

WE KEEP THAT BOOK IN A BIG
WALK-IN CLOSET UP ON THE
MEZZANINE. WE LIKE TO
SIT THERE TO READ IT AND
SCARE OURSELVES TO DEATH.

HUNDREDS
OF **TRUE**
SUPER-WEIRD
STORIES

GHOSTS

UNSOLVED
MURDERS

TRUE UNEXPLAINED STORY #1

THERE'S A STORY ABOUT A KID AND HIS GRANDMOTHER WHO STARTED SEEING HUMAN FACES APPEAR ON THE KITCHEN FLOOR IN THEIR HOUSE. THE FACES LOOKED SAD. THEY TRIED TO WASH THEM AWAY BUT WHEN THEY DID, THE EYES ON THE FACES JUST GREW BIGGER AND SADDER. THE LANDLORD REPLACED THE FLOOR WITH CEMENT, BUT MORE FACES APPEARED, SO THE ROOM WAS PERMANENTLY LOCKED UP. SOME GHOST EXPERTS HID MICROPHONES IN THE KITCHEN, AND THEY RECORDED VOICES WHINING IN UNKNOWN LANGUAGES. NOBODY EVER FOUND AN EXPLANATION TO THE MYSTERY.

TRUE UNEXPLAINED
STORY # 2

THERE'S ANOTHER STORY ABOUT A YOUNG
WOMAN IN THE 1950'S WHO WAS DANCING
WITH HER BOYFRIEND IN LONDON AND SHE
SUDDENLY BURST INTO FLAMES! IN A FEW
SECONDS, SHE WAS DEAD AND TOTALLY
BURNED. THE BOOK SAYS THAT IT HAPPENS TO
SOME PEOPLE: THEY JUST LIGHT UP.

IT'S CALLED SPONTANEOUS COMBUSTION.

THERE ARE MANY MORE STORIES ABOUT

REINCARNATION

PREMONITORY DREAMS

MOVING COFFINS

PEOPLE BURIED ALIVE

PEOPLE WITH MULTIPLE PERSONALITIES

AND OTHER HORRIFYING PHENOMENONS.

SOMETIMES WE PLAY OUIJA.
A OUIJA BOARD HAS LETTERS AND NUMBERS
ON IT AND YES AND NO SIGNS. WE
PUT OUR FINGERS ON A PLASTIC SHAPE
IN THE MIDDLE OF THE BOARD, WE
ASK A QUESTION, AND WE WAIT FOR
THE SHAPE TO START MOVING. IT'S
SUPPOSED TO BE GHOSTS AND SPIRITS
THAT MAKE IT MOVE.

SOMETIMES THE PLASTIC THING WILL ANSWER YES OR NO. SOMETIMES IT SPELLS WORDS. WE LOVE TO ASK THE GHOSTS

SILLY QUESTIONS:

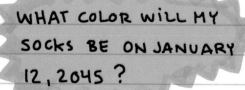

WHAT COLOR WILL MY SOCKS BE ON JANUARY 12, 2045?

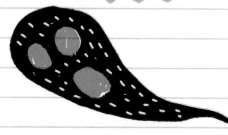

WILL JESSIE GET CAUGHT PICKING HER NOSE IN HIGH SCHOOL?

WE'RE SCARED OF PLAYING NOW, THOUGH,
BECAUSE WE THINK THAT THE WITCH MIGHT
TRY TO MAKE CONTACT WITH US,

THE OTHER NIGHT, AS SOON AS WE PUT
OUR FINGERS ON THE OUIJA PIECE, IT FLEW
OFF AND RAMMED INTO ME, REALLY HARD.
I ALMOST FELL OFF MY CHAIR! WE SCREAMED
SO HARD THAT JULIE'S LITTLE BROTHER, NICK,
STARTED CRYING. JULIE'S MOM CAME AND
PUT THE OUIJA BOARD ON TOP OF THE BOOKSHELF.

SHE SAID THAT OUIJA IS NONSENSE.

IT'S NOT THE SPIRITS
WHO MAKE THE PIECE
MOVE. IT'S YOU, KIDS.
UNCONCIOUSLY.

WE WERE SO FREAKED OUT THAT THE THREE
OF US SLEPT IN THE SAME BED THAT NIGHT.
IT WAS FUN!

THERE'S A BOY NAMED STEVE WHO LIVES NEAR JULIE'S COTTAGE. HE LIVES IN HIS SHACKLIKE HOUSE YEAR-ROUND AND THERE ARE OLD TIRES AND CAR PIECES IN HIS YARD, SO I GUESS HE'S PRETTY POOR.

LAST SUMMER, WE WENT ON A HIKE WITH HIM AND HE SHOWED US GHOST TOWN. IT'S A COUPLE OF ABANDONED SHACKS RIGHT IN THE MIDDLE OF THE WOODS.

THEY'VE BEEN THERE FOR SO LONG THAT TREES ARE GROWING INSIDE THEM. THEY'RE ALL ROTTEN BUT SOME OF THEM STILL HAVE FURNITURE IN THEM. ONE EVEN HAS A FRIDGE!

THERE IS EVEN AN ANCIENT BAR OUT THERE WITH BROKEN CHAIRS AND TABLES AND SOME OLD PITCHERS AND JUGS. IT LOOKS LIKE THE SPOOKY SALOONS IN OLD COWBOY MOVIES. WE LIKE TO IMAGINE SKELETONS AND ZOMBIES DRINKING BEER AND PLAYING CARDS IN THERE AT NIGHT.

STEVE IS ONLY THIRTEEN AND SHOULDN'T DRIVE AN ATV, BUT HE DOES. HIS FATHER DOESN'T CARE. STEVE CAN DO WHATEVER HE WANTS.

THE OTHER DAY AFTER THE OUIJA EPISODE, STEVE CAME OVER TO JULIE'S COTTAGE. HE ASKED IF WE WANTED TO GO FOR A RIDE ON HIS ATV.

I DIDN'T WANT TO. I WAS SCARED. I THOUGHT THAT JULIE'S PARENTS WOULD FREAK OUT IF THEY KNEW WE WENT ON AN ATV DRIVEN BY A KID, AND WITHOUT HELMETS. I KNEW MINE WOULD.

JULIE WANTED TO GO. SHE SAID:
"MY PARENTS DON'T HAVE TO KNOW.

DONT' BE

SUCH A

CHICKEN."

I TURNED AROUND, THINKING THAT JULIE
WOULD'NT DARE TO GO WITH STEVE ALONE,
BUT SHE DID. SHE CLIMBED BEHIND HIM
AND PUT HER ARMS AROUND HIS CHEST
LIKE BIKERS' GIRLFRIENDS IN THE MOVIES
AND THEY LEFT WITHOUT EVEN LOOKING
AT ME.

I WENT BACK INSIDE THE COTTAGE AND
PRETENDED TO READ, BUT I COULD'NT FOCUS
ON THE LETTERS BECAUSE TEARS WERE WELLING
UP IN MY EYES. I FELT LIKE A CHARACTER
FROM A JAPANESE ANIME WITH
RIDICULOUSLY GIANT MANGA EYES FULL
OF WAVES.

JULIE AND STEVE CAME BACK TWO HOURS
LATER AND THEY DIDN'T EVEN TALK TO
ME. THEY PUT ON THEIR BATHING SUITS
AND WENT FOR A DIVE AT THE BIG ROCK.
I COULD HEAR THEIR LAUGHTER ACROSS
THE WATER. I FELT LIKE THE UNIVERSE'S
BIGGEST LOSER.

THAT NIGHT, WE ALL SLEPT IN OUR
SEPARATE BEDS. JULIE KEPT GIVING
ME THE SILENT TREATMENT. SHE
THOUGHT I WAS

BORING.

THE NEXT DAY, WE CAME BACK TO THE
CITY AND WE STILL DIDN'T TALK,
EVEN IN THE CAR.

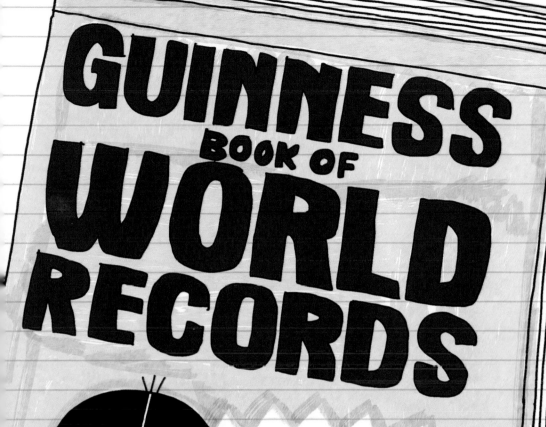

GUINNESS BOOK OF WORLD RECORDS

MOST BORING CHICKEN

EVEN HER BEST FRIEND CAN'T STAND HER!

SO I CAME BACK FROM
JULIE'S COTTAGE WITHOUT
A BEST FRIEND, A WHOLE
SUMMER STRETCHING IN
FRONT OF ME, AND MY
WORST ENEMY TRYING
TO TAKE MY PLACE.

I LIKE TO THINK OF MYSELF AS A PRETTY
INTELLIGENT GIRL, BUT WHEN I'M
ALONE, IT SEEMS LIKE MY BRAIN FOCUSES
ON THE MOST USELESS, STUPID ACTIVITIES,
SUCH AS:

- PAINTING MY TOENAILS GREEN AND
  DRAWING FROG FACES ON THEM
  WITH WITE-OUT

- ORGANIZING PROPER FUNERALS FOR DEAD
  FLIES, COMPLETE WITH HYMNS, EULOGY,
  CRYING, AND BURIAL

- COMPOSING AND RECORDING RAP SONGS
  EXCLUSIVELY WITH FART SOUNDS

- OR LYING DOWN, IMAGINING THAT
  THE HOUSE IS TURNED UPSIDE-DOWN
  AND THAT THE FLOOR IS THE CEILING

  I CAN'T HELP MYSELF. IT'S LIKE MY
  HEAD HAS AN INFINITE CAPACITY
  FOR USELESS PROJECTS.

EVER SINCE WE CAME BACK FROM THE COTTAGE, I'VE HAD A LOT OF TIME FOR ALL OF MY BRAIN'S MONKEY BUSINESS: JULIE IS IGNORING ME. WHEN I CALL HER, SHE'S

ALWAYS BUSY.

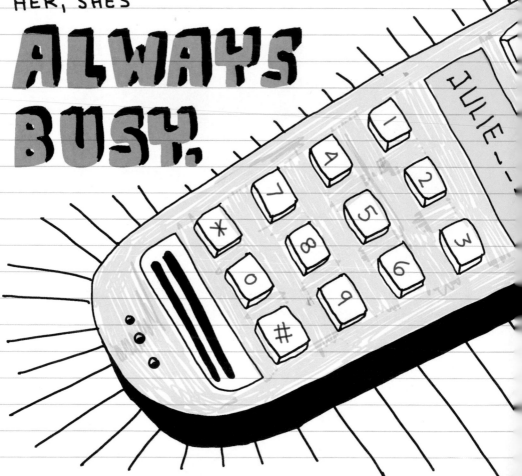

I ENVISIONED THE REST OF MY SUMMER AS A LONG, LONELY ROAD WITH NOTHING TO DO BUT PLAY WITH MY TOES.

A WEEK AFTER WE CAME BACK, THE MOST
DISTURBING THING HAPPENED. ON MY WAY
TO THE MALL, I SAW JULIE ON THE STEPS
OF THE CORNER STORE. WITH NONE OTHER
THAN ISABELLE LEMOINE, DRINKING SLUSHIES.

LAUGHING AT WHAT? MAYBE AT ME.

THEY DIDN'T SEE ME. THAT'S A RELIEF,
BECAUSE I MUST HAVE LOOKED PRETTY
PATHETIC, STANDING THERE ALONE WITH
MY JAW HANGING OPEN.

AS I LEFT, I FELT MY CHEEKS BURN
SO HARD THAT I THOUGHT ABOUT
SPONTANEOUS COMBUSTION. MAYBE
THAT'S HOW THE PHENOMENON STARTS.

THEN I SAW THE FUTURE: JULIE
AND ISABELLE WOULD BE BEST FRIENDS
IN HIGH SCHOOL AND I WOULD FLOAT
THERE ALONE IN THE MIDST OF TWO
THOUSAND UNKNOWN NITWITS.
A REJECT. A NOBODY. I FELT SICK
TO MY STOMACH.

WHY I HATE ISABELLE LEMOINE

💀 💀 💀 💀 💀 💀 💀 💀 💀 💀 💀 💀

(APART FROM THE FACT THAT SHE STOLE MY BEST FRIEND)

- SHE SMOKES AND SHE THINKS IT'S COOL
- SHE SAYS "LIKE" AND "WHATEVER" EVERY THREE WORDS
- SHE HATES ME (WHICH, TO BE HONEST, IS THE MAIN REASON WHY I HATE HER)
- SHE HAS A SCREECHY, HIGH-PITCHED, UGLY VOICE LIKE NAILS SCRATCHING ON A BLACKBOARD
- SHE MAKES FUN OF MY NONEXISTENT BREASTS
- SHE HAS THIN LIPS AND A POINTY BEAK THAT MAKES HER LOOK LIKE AN EAGLE
- SHE'S A CHAMPION ROLLER SKATER AND SHE SKIS AND I'M A CHAMPION AT NOTHING
- SHE WEARS WAAAY TOO MUCH MASCARA
- SHE LIKES TO TORTURE BABY KOALAS (OK, I MADE THAT ONE UP. BUT YOU NEVER KNOW, IT MIGHT BE TRUE.)

WHAT WAS WRONG WITH ME? WHY WOULD JULIE
PREFER THAT STUPID, VAIN ISABELLE? WHAT
WOULD I HAVE TO DO TO BE INTERESTING AND
COOL? WOULD I HAVE TO GET MY NOSE PIERCED?
START SMOKING? DRESS SEXY? ALL THE
OTHER KIDS SEEM TO EITHER BE NATURALLY
COOL OR NOT CARE AT ALL. HOW DO THEY
DO IT? WHY CAN'T I BE LIKE THEM?

EWW! NO WAY!

I TRIED TO DO THINGS ON MY OWN, I FIGURED IT WAS BEST TO GET SOME PRACTICE BECAUSE I WOULD BE SPENDING THE REST OF MY LIFE AS A

misun-derstood

LONER.

I PLAYED WITH MY CAT, OTTAWA.

WHENEVER WE THROW PAPER BALLS FOR HER TO CATCH:

1) SHE STARTS RUNNING AFTER IT LIKE HER TAIL IS ON FIRE, 	**2)** SHE BRAKES ABRUPTLY HALFWAY THERE, SCREECH!
3) SHE FREEZES ON THE SPOT, LOOKING PUZZLED  UH? WHAT WAS I DOING AGAIN?	**4)** THEN SHE STARTS CLEANING HERSELF, PRETENDING THAT WAS HER ORIGINAL INTENTION. WHAT? STOP LOOKING AT ME!

I ALSO PLAYED TRUTH OR DARE WITH TANYA.
SHE MADE ME WALK AROUND THE MALL WITH MY
GUM STUCK TO MY FOREHEAD, AND I MADE HER TAKE
OFF HER SHOES AND COLLECT PENNIES FROM THE
FOUNTAIN IN FRONT OF THE ZELLERS DEPARTMENT STORE.

I ALSO THOUGHT ABOUT THROWING OUT ALL THE THINGS THAT REMIND ME OF MY FRIENDSHIP WITH JULIE, LIKE OUR SUPER-PICKLE COMICS AND OUR PHOTOS.

BUT I DIDN'T. I CAN'T THROW
AWAY STUFF. I MEAN ANYTHING. I
ACTUALLY FEEL SORRY FOR OBJECTS THAT
GET THROWN OUT.

LIST OF THE THINGS THAT I FEEL SORRY FOR:

AS I OFTEN DO WHEN I'M BORED,
I INVENTED A NEW
CHARACTER FOR MYSELF. I HAD
TO REPLACE SUPER-PICKLE.

MY NEW ALTER EGO WAS
CALLED

COYOTITA
THE LONE COYOTE-GIRL!

SHE'S
INDEPENDENT!

SHE'S
MYSTERIOUS!

SHE WEARS
COWBOY BOOTS!

COYOTITA VS SUPER-PICKLE

WAIT A SEC! YOU CAN'T REPLACE AN ALTER-EGO!

FACE IT, KIDDO. YOU'RE ANCIENT HISTORY. TIME TO MOVE ON.

BUT JESSIE NEEDS ME! HOW'S SHE GOING TO FIGHT EVIL NOW?

WE'RE COUNTING ON OUR COOLNESS AND BORED LOOKS TO MAINTAIN A SEMBLANCE OF SUPERIORITY.

I CAN'T BELIEVE THIS! "COOLNESS"! I BET YOU DON'T EVEN FART!

ACTUALLY, I DON'T. I'M WAY TOO MYSTERIOUS.

YOU'RE PATHETIC. YOU'RE NOT EVEN FUNNY!

YEAH, BUT I WEAR COWBOY BOOTS!

I WAS GETTING QUITE ENTHUSIASTIC ABOUT THIS COYOTITA CHARACTER. BUT THEN, LAST WEDNESDAY, AS I WAS READING IN THE STICKS,

JULIE CAME BACK.

I DON'T KNOW WHAT HAPPENED BETWEEN HER AND ISABELLE. THEY HAD A FIGHT, I GUESS.

THE INSULT TOURNAMENT HAD AN UNEASILY TRUE RING TO IT, BUT WE ENDED UP LAUGHING ANYWAY.

SO JULIE AND I MORE OR LESS GOT
BACK TO OUR REGULAR SUMMER
PROGRAM, PART OF WHICH CONSISTED
OF EXPLORING THE MENTAL HOSPITAL.

THE MENTAL HOSPITAL SITS IN THE MIDDLE OF A HUGE PARK BEHIND OUR STREET. IT'S ALL FENCED IN, BUT WE GET INTO THE PARK BY CLIMBING THE FENCE NEXT TO THE TOOLSHED IN MY BACKYARD.

THINGS WE FOUND
IN THE HOSPITAL PARK:

- A CORNFIELD (PERFECT FOR PLAYING HIDE AND SEEK)
- A VEGETABLE PATCH
- A BARN WITH FARMING EQUIPMENT
- A CUTE POND WITH GOLDFISH AND DUCKS (PERFECT FOR DAYDREAMING ABOUT BEN)
- HENS! (I'M NOT KIDDING)
- A TOWER THAT LOOKS LIKE A CASTLE TOWER BUT THAT'S REALLY AN OLD WATER TANK
- AN ABANDONED MINI- GOLF COURSE ALL COVERED IN WEEDS THAT WE CALL:

THERE'S ALSO A PLAYGROUND, WITH SWINGS, CLIMBING
ROPES AND ALL, AND EVERYTHING IS <u>ADULT SIZED</u>!!!
WE'VE NEVER SEEN ANY PATIENTS PLAYING THERE
AND FRANKLY I'M THANKFUL FOR THAT BECAUSE

THAT
WOULD
BE REALLY
CREEPY.

THE HOSPITAL ITSELF IS PRETTY OLD. IT WAS BUILT IN 1873. I GUESS THAT'S WHY SOME PARTS OF IT LOOK LIKE A FAIRY TALE CASTLE.

I FOUND A BOOK ABOUT THE HOSPITAL AT THE LIBRARY. EMILE NELLIGAN, A FAMOUS FRENCH-CANADIAN POET, SPENT A BIG PART OF HIS LIFE THERE. HE WAS AWFULLY CUTE.

ONCE, THERE WAS A YARD SALE AT THE HOSPITAL AND MY MOM BOUGHT AN OLD UPRIGHT PIANO FOR $20. IT WAS COVERED WITH CIGARETTE BURNS AND COFFEE STAINS. I LIKE TO THINK THAT MAYBE EMILE NELLIGAN PLAYED ON IT.

SOMETIMES, I IMAGINE I LIVE IN 1910 AND I'M A NURSE WORKING AT THE HOSPITAL, AND I HELP EMILE ESCAPE BECAUSE I FIND OUT HE'S NOT CRAZY AT ALL, JUST DIFFERENT. AND THEN OF COURSE, HE FALLS IN LOVE WITH ME AND WE MARRY AND WE WRITE POETRY TOGETHER.

NO ONE THIS CUTE CAN BE CRAZY FOR REAL.

WHEN WE PLAY IN THE PARK, WE'RE MOSTLY ALONE. SOMETIMES WE MEET WITH A GROUP OF PATIENTS TAKING A WALK WITH AN AIDE. THE PATIENTS ALWAYS LOOK SLUMPED WITH DARK CIRCLES UNDER THEIR EYES AND TEETH YELLOWED BY CIGARETTE SMOKE. THEY ALL LOOK OLD, EVEN THE YOUNG ONES.

NONE OF THEM LOOK LIKE EMILE NELLIGAN.

SOME OF THEM BITE THEIR OWN FIST OR ROCK THEMSELVES ENDLESSLY. SOME OF THEM MOAN OR MUTTER OR SCREAM.

HOW DO PEOPLE BECOME CRAZY?

DOES IT BEGIN BY ACTING
A LITTLE STRANGE, LIKE
INVENTING CHARACTERS FOR
YOURSELF OR TALKING TO
YOUR CAT?

CRAZY PEOPLE SCARE ME.

BUT NOTHING IN THE PARK IS AS SCARY AS

THE BLUE
VAN.

THE BLUE VAN

THE BLUE VAN IS THE HOSPITAL'S SECURITY
VAN. IT'S THERE TO MAKE SURE THE
PATIENTS DON'T GET OUT OF THE HOSPITAL
AND THAT KIDS LIKE US DON'T GET <u>IN</u>.
WE'VE NEVER SEEN THE BLUE VAN'S
DRIVER. BUT EVERY TIME WE SEE THE
VAN LURKING AROUND THE FIELD, WE
RUN AWAY LIKE A BUNCH OF ANTELOPES.

MIKE TOLD US THAT ONE OF HIS COUSINS WAS
CAUGHT PLAYING IN THE HAUNTED MINI-PUTT
ONCE AND THE GUARDS IN THE BLUE VAN LOCKED
HIM IN THE HOSPITAL'S BASEMENT FOR THE NIGHT.
WE KNOW THAT'S WHERE THEY PUT THE DANGEROUS
PATIENTS BECAUSE WE CAN SEE PADDED CELLS
THROUGH TINY WINDOWS IN A WALL ON THE
EASTERN SIDE OF THE HOSPITAL.

APPARENTLY, MIKE'S COUSIN WAS FED DEAD
SPIDERS AND WATER, AND WHEN THEY RELEASED
HIM, THEY TOLD HIM THAT IF HE WAS CAUGHT IN
THE PARK AGAIN, THEY WOULD HAVE TO USE

ELECTROTHERAPY!

RIP
MIKE'S
COUSIN

DIED
FROM PLAYING
MINI-PUTT
IN THE
WRONG
PLACE

SO THE OTHER DAY, WHILE WE WERE CLIMBING
THE BIG PINE TREE NEAR THE BARN, THE BLUE
VAN APPEARED FROM BEHIND THE TOOLSHED.

THE OTHERS RAN OFF AND MANAGED TO CLIMB
THE FENCE, BUT I WAS A FEW BRANCHES HIGHER
AND DIDN'T HAVE TIME TO GET DOWN.

THE BLUE VAN STOPPED BELOW THE TREE, AND
THE DOOR OPENED. IF I WERE A CHARACTER
IN A CHEESY BOOK, I WOULD SAY

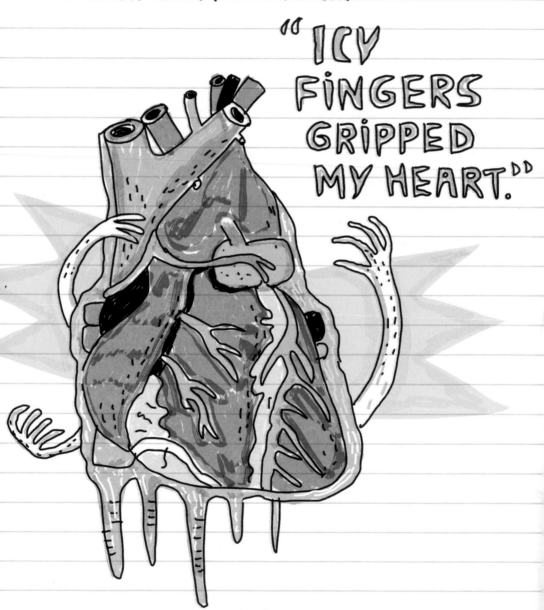

"ICY FINGERS GRIPPED MY HEART."

A MAN CAME OUT. I LOOKED AROUND AND
THE OTHERS WERE GONE.

THE MAN SAID:

THEN I HEARD BEN'S VOICE. HE WAS STANDING
NEXT TO ME AND TOUCHED MY ELBOW.
I THOUGHT HE'D ESCAPED WITH THE OTHERS.
HERE'S WHAT I HEARD.

 — WE'RE LEAVING. COME ON, SIR, WE WON'T
COME BACK, I PROMISE.

 — WELL, LOOK AT THIS: A HERO. AREN'T YOU
THE KID FROM THE TRANSMISSION SHOP?

 BEN DIDN'T ANSWER. HIS DAD OWNS THE
TRANSMISSION SHOP AT THE END OF OUR STREET.

 — EVER WONDER WHY YOU SEE THOSE PICTURES
OF MISSING KIDS? PROBABLY HAREBRAINED
ONES LIKE YOU, PLAYING AROUND DERANGED
PEOPLE. NOW CLEAR OFF BEFORE I TAKE YOU BACK
TO YOUR DAD MYSELF.

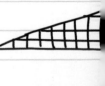

ONCE SAFE ON THE OTHER SIDE OF THE
FENCE, BEN AND I SAT ON THE TOP OF
MY GARDEN SHED. WE ATE SOME
COOKIES THAT I KEEP HIDDEN IN A
HOLE UNDER A LOOSE SHINGLE, AND
WE TALKED A BIT ABOUT WHAT THE
MAN HAD SAID ABOUT THE MISSING
KIDS.

LAST JUNE, A GIRL OUR AGE WENT
MISSING IN BROSSARD. WE
STILL SEE THE POSTERS AT THE
CORNER STORE, IN FRONT OF THE
CHURCH, THE LIQUOR STORE, AND
AT THE COUNTER IN FRANCINE'S
SNACK BAR. THE GIRL HASN'T
BEEN FOUND YET.

BEN SAID: "THAT GUY SURE
LOOKED LIKE A MANIAC.
MAYBE HE'S THE ONE PICKING
UP KIDS IN HIS VAN."

HE WAS KIDDING, OF COURSE, BUT
WE STILL MANAGED TO GET ALL
FREAKED OUT ABOUT IT.

THIS WAS THE LONGEST CONVERSATION
I'VE HAD WITH BEN IN MY WHOLE

LIFE.

QUESTION: DO MANIACS ALWAYS LOOK LIKE MANIACS?

CAN'T A MANIAC LOOK LIKE

THIS →

OR THIS ↓

OR THIS ?

AND FRANKLY, ISN'T A CUTE MANIAC EVEN SCARIER THAN AN UGLY MANIAC?

DISCOVERY:

BEING SCARED WITH
BEN IS A LOT MORE
FUN THAN BEING
SCARED ALONE.
★ ★ ★

WE ALWAYS PLAY TOGETHER AT RECESS. HE'S BETTER AT SOCCER BUT I'M BETTER AT STRATEGO.

HIS FRIENDS ARE PISSED OFF WHEN HE PLAYS WITH ME INSTEAD OF PLAYING DODGEBALL WITH THEM, BUT HE DOESN'T CARE.

AFTER SCHOOL, WE LIKE TO HANG OUT ON THE HILL NEAR THE RAILROAD TRACKS. WE CAN SEE THE OIL REFINERIES FROM THERE. THEY LOOK LIKE MANHATTAN AT NIGHT, WITH ALL THE LIGHTS AND SMOKE. SOMETIMES WE SIT THERE FOR HOURS.

THINGS MOST PEOPLE FIND PRETTY

- PONIES
- BUTTERFLIES
- ROSES
- UNICORNS

THINGS BEN AND I FIND PRETTY:

- CENTIPEDES
- PRAYING MANTISES
- COYOTES
- REFINERIES

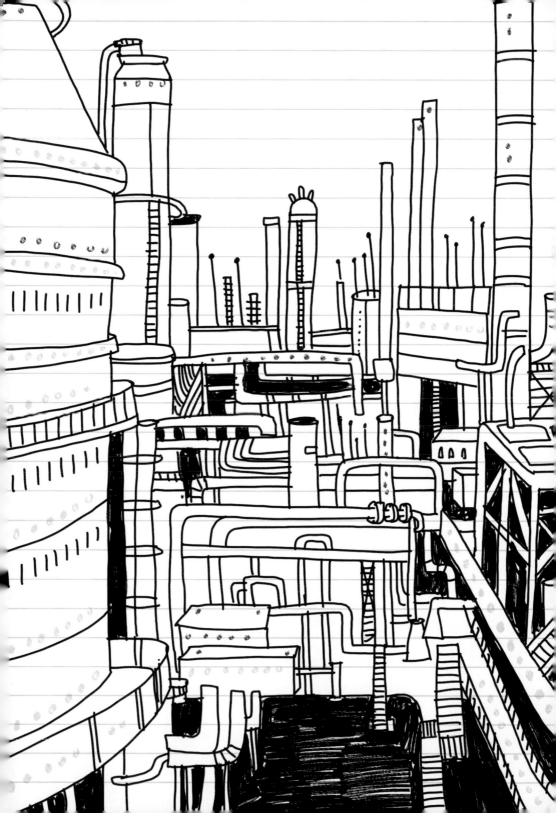

I'VE KNOW THE GUY FOREVER, AND
JUST LATELY, I STARTED GETTING
ALL SHY AND SILLY AND BABBLY
AROUND HIM.

SO EVEN THOUGH IT WAS SCARY, THE BLUE
VAN EPISODE WAS A GOOD THING IN A WAY
BECAUSE NOW I KNOW THAT BEN CARES
FOR ME.

BLAHBLAH BLAHBLAH
BLAH BLAHBLAH BLAHBLAH
BLAH BLAHBLAH BLAHBLAH
BLAH BLAHBLAH BLAHBLAH BLAHBLAH
BLAH BLAHBLAH BLAHBLAH BLAHBLAH
BLAHBLAH BLAHBLAH BLAHBLAH BLAHBLAH BLAHBLAH
BLAHBLAH BLAHBLAH BLAHBLAH BLAHBLAH BLAHBLAH BLAHBLAH
BLAHBLAH BLAHBLAH BLAHBLAH BLAHBLAH BLAHBLAH BLAHBLAH

THE ONLY
PROBLEM
WAS, RIGHT
AFTER THAT,
BEN
DISAPPEARED.

FOUR DAYS AFTER THE BLUE VAN EPISODE,
I HADN'T SEEN BEN ONCE! I GUESS I
STARTED WORRYING THE EVENING I
WAS BABYSITTING WITH JULIE.

JULIE AND I, WE BABYSIT TOGETHER
A LOT, AND WE HAVE A SOFT SPOT FOR
STRANGE KIDS.

 THAT NIGHT, WE WERE BABY-SITTING FRANCIS AND HE WAS ALREADY IN BED. WE WERE CHATTING

WHAT I HOPED JULIE WOULD SAY:

BEN STAYED WITH YOU. THAT'S GOOD. IT'S PROOF THAT HE LIKES YOU.

AND EATING FRITOS AND I TOLD JULIE
ABOUT BEN COMING TO MY RESCUE WITH THE BLUE
VAN MAN.

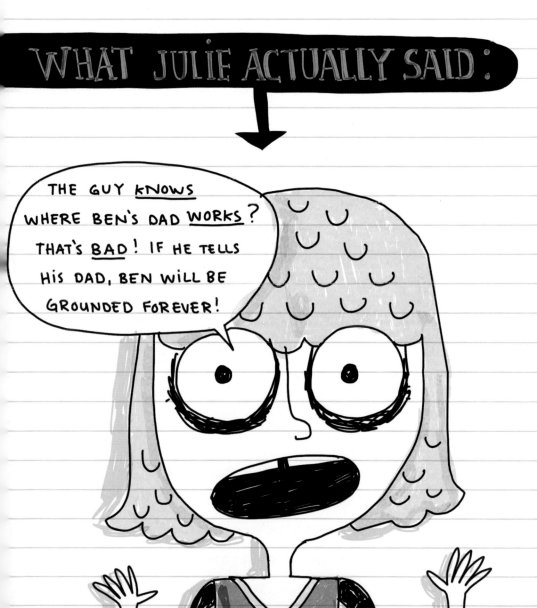

IT DAWNED ON ME THEN,
THAT'S WHY I HADN'T SEEN
BEN FOR DAYS. HE WAS
IN TROUBLE. HE WAS IN
TROUBLE BECAUSE OF

HERE I WAS STUPIDLY THINKING
THAT HE LIKED ME WHILE HE
WAS PROBABLY GROUNDED AND
LOCKED UP IN HIS ROOM AND
CURSING ME FOR BEING SUCH A
HELPLESS NITWIT.

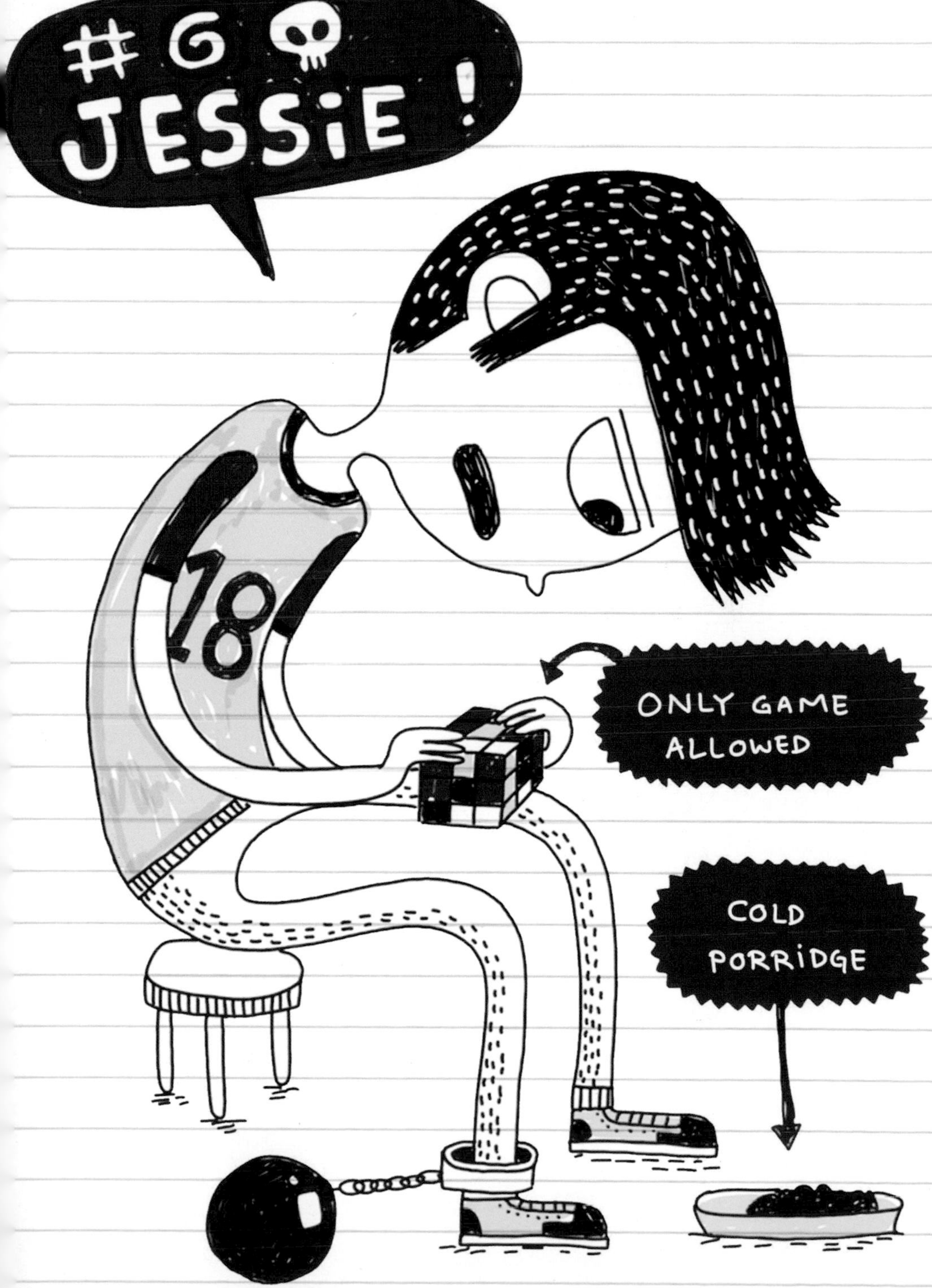
#6
JESSiE !
18
ONLY GAME ALLOWED
COLD PORRiDGE

OR
worse!

I REMEMBERED WHAT THE
BLUE VAN MAN HAD SAID
ABOUT DISAPPEARING KIDS.
I SUDDENLY FELT COLD ALL
OVER.

"YOU HAVE TO TALK TO HIM
AND FIND OUT!", JULIE SAID.
BUT I DIDN'T DARE CALL
BEN'S HOME IN CASE HIS DAD
ANSWERED.

I AM AFRAID OF MY FRIEND'S PARENTS.

OK, BUT LET'S ADMIT THAT GIANT UNIBROWS DON'T HELP.

So we went on a quest to find Ben. I was glad that Julie was with me. It kind of made up for letting me down after the cottage fight. Plus, it felt good to have a boy expert by my side.

We looked everywhere for two days:

- The mall's arcade
- The park
- The soccer field
- The corner store steps
- The alley behind Ben's dad's garage
- The movie theater
- The sticks
- The haunted mini-putt
- Mike's backyard

BEN DIDN'T SHOW UP,

I FELT SO GUILTY. I KEPT THINKING; SHOULD I CALL THE POLICE? BUT SURELY IF BEN HAD DISAPPEARED, HIS PARENTS WOULD HAVE ASKED US QUESTIONS?

BEN WAS PROBABLY JUST GROUNDED OR STUCK IN BED WITH A STOMACH FLU AND I WOULD LOOK RIDICULOUS IF I ALERTED THE AUTHORITIES.

THERE WAS ALSO THE POSSIBILITY THAT BEN SIMPLY GOT BORED WITH ME AND THAT HE WAS JUST STEERING CLEAR OF MY INCESSANT BABBLING. UNFORTUNATELY, COPS AREN'T TRAINED TO PROTECT KIDS AGAINST FRIENDS DUMPING THEM.

I COULDN'T FIND A WAY TO CALM DOWN.

CALMING DOWN IS CLEARLY NOT MY
BEST STRENGTH. HERE'S THE GENERAL STATE OF

MY INNARDS:

SERIOUSLY
THAT WOULD
← MAKE A
REALLY COOL
T-SHIRT

THEN YESTERDAY MORNING, THERE WAS
AN AIRMAIL ENVELOPE STUCK WITH
DUCT TAPE TO THE BAR OF MY BIKE,

IN THE ENVELOPE, A MESSAGE
SAID:

HEY JESSIE, HOW ARE YOU,
I JUST GOT BACK FROM SOCCER
CAMP. IT WAS GREAT, WE
NEVER TOOK SHOWERS, WE JUST
WASHED IN THE LAKE! I SAW
TWO RACCOONS. HERE'S A
NECKLACE I MADE FOR YOU WITH
A PENNY THAT I LEFT ON THE
RAILROAD TRACK. A TRAIN
FLATTENED IT. ISN'T IT COOL?

BEN

HE WAS JUST AT CAMP! HE WASN'T
ABDUCTED! HE WASN'T GROUNDED!
HE DOESN'T HATE ME!

HE MADE A NECKLACE FOR ME WITH A FLATTENED PENNY!

THIS IS THE COOLEST, CUTEST, PRETTIEST, MOST ADORABLE NECKLACE EVER!!!

I STARTED RUNNING AROUND LIKE A
HEADLESS CHICKEN AND THEN
EVENTUALLY ENDED UP AT JULIE'S
PLACE, SHOWING HER THE LETTER.

"COOL", JULIE SAID. "DOES IT MEAN

HOW

ARE YOU SUPPOSED TO

FIND OUT

IF YOU ARE

GOING OUT

WITH

SOMEONE?

ASK?

DECLARE YOUR LOVE?

HOLD HANDS?

OR EVEN WORSE... KISS?

BECAUSE <u>YES</u>, OF COURSE
I'M A BIT SCARED OF KISSES.
NOT SUPER-SCARED, BUT
A BIT <u>DISGUSTED-SCARED</u>.

WHAT IF THE PERSON YOU
KISS HASN'T BRUSHED HIS
TEETH FOR A WEEK?

WHAT IF HE'S JUST EATEN
SALT & VINEGAR CHIPS AND
TASTES GROSS?

WHEN JULIE AND I WERE DONE
GIGGLING ABOUT KISSING
ISSUES, WE SPENT THE MORNING
ORGANIZING OUR BACKPACKS
AND SELECTING OUR OUTFITS FOR
THE FIRST DAY OF SCHOOL,
WHICH IS NEXT WEEK. WE
DO THAT TOGETHER EVERY YEAR
AND IT'S KIND OF FUN. WE
LIKE GETTING MATCHING BACKPACKS
AND WE DECORATE OUR
PENCIL CASES WITH SUPER-PICKLE
DOODLES.

WE ALWAYS DRESS A BIT ALIKE. NOT
ENTIRELY LIKE WE USED TO IN FIRST
GRADE, BUT WITH MATCHING ELEMENTS.
HERE'S WHAT WE CHOSE THIS TIME:

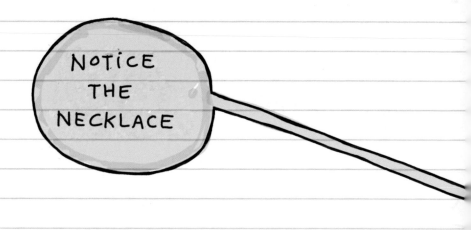

DRESSED FOR SUCCESS!
THE BEATLES
IMAGINE
I ALWAYS DREAMED OF WEARING A QUILT!

THEN WE HAD LUNCH, AND IN
THE AFTERNOON, BEN AND I
TOOK OUR BIKES AND WE
WENT TO SIT ON THE HILL IN FRONT
OF THE REFINERIES.

THE AIR SMELLED LIKE THE INSIDE
OF A NEW CAR, AND CANNED PEAS,
AND ALSO OF GRASS AND THE
ROTTEN MUD FROM THE RIVER NOT
FAR. IT FELT LIKE THE PERFECT
SMELL. IT SMELLED LIKE THE
END OF AUGUST.

HE DIDN'T KISS ME OR ANYTHING.
WE JUST SAT THERE TRYING TO LIST
OUR TOP 10 OF THE SILLIEST JOKES WE
EVER HEARD.

OUR NUMBER 1:

SO THERE'S TWO MUFFINS IN THE
OVEN. ONE MUFFIN LOOKS OVER
AND SAYS; "JEEZ IT'S GETTING
HOT IN HERE". THE OTHER MUFFIN
SAYS "OH MY GOSH, A
TALKING MUFFIN !"

BEFORE WE LEFT, WE STUCK OUR
GUM NEXT TO EACH OTHER'S
UNDER THE BENCH AND DECIDED
WE'D COME BACK NEXT SUMMER
AND SEE IF IT'S STILL THERE.

WHAT WILL HAPPEN TO ME IN THE MEANTIME? HERE ARE SOME
POSSIBILITIES:

POPULARITY

BREASTS

COWBOY BOOTS

GOLD MEDAL OF THE FASTEST ARCHIE READER

MY EARS GETTING MAGICALLY SMALLER

GETTING FAMOUS FOR MY COMIC ART GENIUS

SUPER PICKLE

OR i COULD END UP BEING
THE EXACT SAME GOOD OL'
JESSIE ELLIOT, WHICH, I GUESS...